Liquid Courage-An Indigenous Scifi Short Story

Liquid Courage

It was going to take more than tobacco to burn through the bad vibes in Jessie's cubicle. Better yet she'd like a glass or two of wine to smooth over her frazzled nerves, and help her creativity flow.

The company claimed to celebrate "diversity," but the only concession she was allowed to her heritage was the beadwork inspired screensaver on her computer terminal and the ability to wear her black hair in a long braid. She had to settle for placing a small leather pouch of tobacco in her jacket pocket and clutching it as her immediate supervisor, Hank, spoke to her.

Hank often assigned her ad campaigns no one else wanted to do. She would've passed on "Lucidity" too if Hank had let her.

"I'm not into gaming. I've never been into gaming. I wouldn't know how to reach these people." She clutched at the tobacco in her pocket as she said this.

"They want to appeal to a new demographic that doesn't play games," Hank began. "This is an app that'll challenge its players to learn new facts or skills so they can form the extra neurons they'll need to stave off dementia later."

"Oh—that doesn't sound too bad," Jessie sighed in

relief. "It sounds no worse than multimedia software they have to help teach kids."

"Yeah, you can log unto this URL on your smartphone, and get familiar with the app, so you can come up with good sales pitches for it," Hank said. "You're free to spend the rest of the afternoon playing Lucidity."

Jessie nodded. When he left she played Lucidity. There were card games, matching games and mathematical skill testing games. Each time she won there was the sound of applause. It was cute at first, but started to get annoying.

She saw a movement out of the corner of her eye. She looked up and saw that Trudy was looking through the cubicle door at her. "Must be nice," she snorted.

Trudy's friend Angie was nearby and tittered at this.

Jessie was about to say, "research," but neither of them gave her a chance to do so before they headed off for one of their long coffee breaks. It was ridiculous to feel like she'd been busted, but she still logged into her mailbox to review her incoming email as a more socially acceptable task, Let Liquid Courage change your life!

Liquid Courage already has an established place in my life! She felt like replying to the spammer, and would've if she were at home on her "Rezgrrl" accounts. She was about to delete the message when she saw the sender was Ashton

Levine, the company's top producer, Did you send this message? You better check to see if you've got malware.

She was about to run a virus scan when she received a reply from Ashton, Y r u saying that?

She texted back, I got an ad for 'Liquid Courage' from your work account.

Ashton: So u thought my opening was spam? No wonder y I keep getting notices that the email has been deleted and no 1 admits to reading it! : /

Jessie shuddered in disgust: I hope u haven't sent this out to customers?

I haven't, but there's no telling what the company did before they consulted with me. Why don't we see how we mesh over lunch? How does 12:30 @ Kelsing's sound 2 u?

Jessie believed she worked best when she worked with a buzz though she stopped short of drinking herself into a blackout. The prospect of a liquid lunch appealed to her, so she texted back, I'll b there.

Kelsing's was the most exclusive restaurant in the City, so Jessie had high hopes there'd be a good bar there.

Ashton was texting away on his smartphone when she got to their table. Jessie shook her head. Just when Jessie assumed that she'd be ignored he looked up and smiled at her, "Let's get some drinks."

"I'd like a beer," he said to a nearby server.

"I'll have a glass of wine," Jessie said as she sat down.

Ashton reached for his tablet as soon as she sat down, "I asked you out, so I can ask your professional opinion on my Liquid Courage campaign. I have to warn you that the technical details of the product is dry, but I feel this product has the possibility of taking off if it gets the right push."

He gave Jessie the tablet and called up the PDFs and documents he was working on. Jessie looked at his list of pitches first instead of the prospectus in the hope that it'd give her the gist of Liquid Courage.

You may not have social anxiety disorder, but you get severe stage fright when you have to perform in front of an audience. Would you like the confidence you need to handle large crowds and parties? Liquid Courage can help you take things up to the next level and improve your performance.

"Hmm," Jessie said.

"What do you think?" Ashton asked.

"It reads like spam for a brewing company. You're better off showing a bunch of people partying than this," Jessie sniffed.

"I'm not selling liquor. I'm selling pharmaceuticals

for 'voluntary Briggs–Meyer reassignment'."

"Oh," Jessie said slowly.

"Which is basically turning introverts into extroverts. They don't have extreme social anxiety, but are too quiet to get ahead," Ashton added when he assumed she didn't know what he meant.

Jessie stroked her chin. "Hmm."

"You think there's a market for it?" he asked.

"Yeah—–but they wouldn't want to be party animals. Just

a little bolder," she mused to herself. "I figure you should add images where worthwhile goals are out of reach, but don't present them as if they're Vegas jackpots."

Ashton input all of her words into his smartphone.

"Or just have a commercial start out in black and white, but then shift it into technicolor. Don't make the black and white images depressing. Have it be a lovely scene in beautiful settings so that the inclusion of color gives it a richness and depth that was missing before. That should work for the casual viewer.

If you want to attract a young professional who is introverted show them thinking on their feet during an interview or a question and answer session."

Ashton nodded and smiled at all the ideas he recorded, "This is good."

He grimaced, "Only thing is I don't know what would be 'overkill'.

"Overkill?" Jessie asked.

"You know how to get the attention of an introvert who is as busy as everyone else in the modern age without scaring them off with sudden noises. I'd like to offer you a part of the commission and bonus I'll get for a successful campaign if you'll collaborate with me," Ashton said.

"What do you have in mind?' Jessie asked.

"I was wondering if you could start with a website

evaluation, and we'll go from there," Ashton said.

"I appreciate you thinking of me, Ashton, but I really don't have time for this. I've already got another project I'm working on," she began.

"Trudy said you were experiencing a slow period right now," Ashton grinned archly.

Jessie sighed. "Hank's got me working on a pet project of his. He believes that giving me free samples helps my creativity."

"In that case, why don't you use this coupon? I can load an app for a coupon code on your smartphone," Ashton said. He texted her the code.

"You have a lot of faith in Liquid Courage's future?" Jessie asked.

She laughed. "They must already be doing a good job advertising their product if they've won you over. How come no one's heard of it before?" Jessie asked.

"It was a family secret that was only offered to a select

few, but now they are willing to offer it to the public," Ashton said.

"At least review the website for us to optimize views? I can make sure that a consultant's fee for you is added to the final invoice," Ashton said.

Jessie sighed. "I can give you one afternoon of my time to take a quick look at the site and give you feedback. I can't guarantee that it will be a magic bullet for Liquid Courage."

On the way back to the office she wished she'd given a firm "no" instead of giving Ashton this much. She already had her own assignment and didn't need any more work.

Lucidity took up her company time. Liquid Courage would have to take up her private time since the only reason she'd agreed to do this was much was because she found the idea of Liquid Courage personally intriguing.

An alarm went off when she went to check out

their website for further investigation: You can be a winner! You've hit the jackpot from now on! Don't let this opportunity pass you by!

Heavy metal pounded out of the speakers as if she were at a concert. She would've thought it a better ad if it were for "High Octane" instead of "Liquid Courage" and typed the comment into her Ipad. Images flashed too fast for her to make sense of them. Mostly feats of athleticism so that she wrote down, Is this an ad for steroids? You'll have people thinking Liquid Courage is dangerous and illegal! At least that's what the introverts will be thinking, and they are the demographic you're trying to sell to.

A tab of testimonials caught her eye. She went through them one by one. The first testimonial was narrated by a woman with her before and after pictures. "I used to volunteer at the community theater, but was too shy to actually be on the stage. I was a set designer. Thanks to Liquid Courage I was the opening act, and even did an impromptu stand up act."

The image was grainy, but a man stood up and snorted, "What's all this talk about your "vajajay?" Are you postal or premenstrual?"

"Either works for me," the woman snapped in the middle of a monologue.

Jessie snickered at this and typed, This is a good example of thinking on your feet, but I feel that an introvert would want to maintain professional courtesy.

"I need to put myself out there! I keep being outstaged!" Another man growled into the camera. Then he was practically screaming on a stage so loud that Jessie couldn't make out the words. She shook her head, and wrote on the Ipad, Are there various packages for the customer to choose from? Grouping the testimonials for the package a customer wants would make more sense in such a case. It'd be wise to show the full range, so as not to drive away someone who wants a lesser dosage of "Liquid Courage."

"This stuff is pure gold," Ashton said at their next lunch meeting. "I sent your suggestions to the website admin, and he's already tweaked the design according to what you said. They've already experienced a 200%

increase in the number of self referrals they received."

Jessie's brows rose. "Liquid Courage's staff works fast."

"Of course, a fast turnaround time is their biggest selling feature!" Ashton grinned. "They believe in their product and are the main shareholders."

"Do they list the side effects?" Jessie asked. His expression made her add, "It's a requirement."

"Before they sign on the dotted line yes. Our job is

to pique people's interest. It's the buyer's job to do due diligence," Ashton shrugged.

Jessie sighed. " Maybe, but I wouldn't feel comfortable to market a shoddy product."

The corners of Ashton's mouth twitched almost as if in laughter.

Jessie hoped they were on the up and up. She hoped the sensationalistic advertising was a sign of bad marketing and not of an inferior product.

It'd be cool if I could be Rezgrrl all the time. Maybe Liquid Courage could help me if I took a chance on it?

Hank often had her try out their customers' products to better understand their unique selling points for their potential customers. Liquid Courage sounded like it was worth trying out.

The ad copy for "Liquid Courage" reminded her of her early use of alcohol when she was younger. Most times her binges were motivated by the desire to nerve herself to do something that made her nervous. Nowadays, she imbibed mostly when she wanted to update her Rezgrrl social media accounts.

"Liquid Courage" might let her access that part of her personality without having to drink alcohol and she was itching to try it.

Any other place or product and Jessie would've left as soon as she saw the inside of the clinic's office. Not only had they hired a poor marketer they'd paid for a bad interior decorator. She could understand that they didn't want to be staid and boring, but their office's choice of colors was enough to induce vertigo or epileptic fits in the sensitive.

"I'm Jessie Maracle. I'm here for my three o'clock appointment," Jessie said to the receptionist who had a shock of cherry red spikes on her head. The name plaque on her desk read "Cherise."

The girl clapped her hands so loudly that the bangles on her arms gave off their own chimes, "Oh, you're the Miracle Worker! You know we've had 200% increase in business and the numbers keep climbing since you helped our web admin optimize our website, and coordinate our outreach for our various packages."

Cherise's grin was as brilliant as a neon sign.

Jessie laughed, "I'd rather be 'Rezgrrl' than a 'Miracle Worker.'"

"We can help you be whatever or whoever you want to be," Cherise nodded.

Cherise rang a bell.

Jessie jumped when a voice barked, "What is it?" "You're three o'clock appointment is here!" Cherise retorted in a similar tone.

There was a loud sigh. "Send them in."

"Hmm," Jessie muttered as she was ushered down the hall.

Jessie didn't know if she was entering a private booth in a dance club or else a doctor's office. The chrome was so shiny it gave off rainbows. Dr. Phoenix's name plate was rendered in holographic print.

"We need to ask you a series of questions, so we can customize our treatment program for you, Ms. Maracle," Dr. Phoenix said.

"Do you wish to break the ice or to let loose?" Dr. Phoenix snapped.

"I'd have alcohol binges if I wanted to 'let loose'." Jessie said.

Dr. Phoenix grimaced, "Do not mix Liquid Courage with alcohol!"

"I'm hoping to substitute Liquid Courage for alcohol," Jessie said.

"Liquid Courage is NOT an intoxicant!" Dr. Phoenix snapped.

"I'm not looking for intoxication. I'm want to get the inhibitions that block my creativity lowered without the risk of cirrhosis," Jessie said.

Dr. Phoenix typed notes rapidly in her tablet, "You want performance enhancement."

"What is your occupation?" She glanced at her notes before Jessie had a chance to respond.

"Oh! You're the Miracle Worker! You've already tripled our business. I'd like to see what you can do under the influence of Liquid Courage!" She paused for a microsecond, "Tell you what. We'll give you a month's supply as a bonus! I want to see what you can do for us when you've got Liquid Courage in your fuel tank!"

"Wow—that's generous of you," Jessie said.

"Liquid Courage comes in liquid caplets. Take one a day. The effects are cumulative," Dr. Phoenix said. "When you have reached the level of performance you desire maintain the effects by taking one pill a week."

Jessie looked at the prescription order if as it were a stick of dynamite. She didn't know whether she was scared or excited by the possibilities.

She logged onto her favorite sites after taking her first pill at home. To her that meant that she rated different websites for stickiness. She started with the better ones as prime examples of what to do. Beautiful graphics, user-friendliness, premium content. The only common theme was how effectively they showcased their chosen product. I couldn't do better myself. was the biggest compliment she could give a site.

When she posted her views on Rezgrrl she added the disclaimer, Note: I am rating these sites by the effectiveness of their promotions, not the value of the products they sell. That may seem shallow, but there's many worthy products/causes that have failed because of poor marketing and I seek to educate the public on how to sell their wares.

She added on impulse, I'm free for a two hour group chat tomorrow night at 7–9 p.m. Why don't you submit your URLs and I'll give you a quick comments on them?

Jessie had the impulse to redecorate her cubicle at work. She went to a stationary store to buy Keep Out, Do Not Disturb and Be Back signs. She often heard mutterings of Indian Time if she didn't account for every minute of her time on the job, yet often had to put up with constant interruptions in her work. She wanted to see if she'd get more done if she had fewer interruptions. She planned to put the signs up on an as needed basis.

"Humph," Trudy said when she went up to the door of her cubicle to inspect the rumored changes herself.

The new signs gave Jessie enough time to read Lucidity's prospectus in its entirety. She used a red highlighter, and added notes to the document.

Learning isn't only for the young. The young need to learn to grow. The old need to learn in order maintain their mental health....POLISH YOUR MARBLES SO YOU DON'T LOSE YOUR MARBLES!

She snickered at this. Then continued to write in a stream of consciousness. Why should you engage in a self study program for your neurons unless you're afraid that they're not what they used to be? You should be able to share your results if you reach a high score!....Self study is boring. Make it a team sport!

The words kept flowing and flowing. More and faster than they had before. She stopped when she reached the end of the page. This was the best flow she'd ever had ! She went home with a feeling of accomplishment. She couldn't wait to see what happened on Rezgrrl that night!

That night there was a message asking her opinion of a porno site when she logged in for the chat. Jessie glanced at the still of the video in her link and wrote back to the troll, What demographic do you cater to, the fugly?

The troll sent back, Is this more to your liking?

Only if I was into rubber dolls, Loser!

A third party in the chat commented, Word of Advice Rezgrrl: don't feed trolls. Report and block them.

Jessie took their advice, and the rest of the chat went smoothly.

She used links to her earliest work as a more PC examples of what not to do.

A "Minnie Sparrow" sent a link to her site, and asked for a free site evaluation when it was time for her to log off the chatroom. The site was a textbook example of what not to do. It was little more than a sloppily edited, virtual postcard and price list with a picture of someone's Grandma on it. One comment wasn't enough to suffice, and the words kept flowing and flowing out of her.

She uploaded screenshots of the website with each

comment, and when she was done for the night she logged off the chatroom.

The first thing she saw at work was a message from her immediate supervisor, Our client wants to see our progress on their campaign. Send me what you've done so far.

Jessie typed all the comments she'd made with the Lucidity prospectus into a single document that she emailed him.

At lunch, he sent back the response, What is this? It's not up to your usual standards. I can't send this to our client. It's an insult to Lucidity's potential customers.

You have until tomorrow morning to send me something I can use, or you're off the project...

Jessie cussed, but the words were garbled on her tongue. She was so frustrated by her lack of articulation that

her vision became red, and
she screamed in rage instead.

Trudy came up to Jessie's
cubicle with a bottle of pills
in hand, "This will deal with
the cramps, if the pains got
you feeling grumpy, but PMS
is no excuse to be less than
professional!"

She placed them on
Jessie's desk. Jessie took the
bottle and pelted it back
to Trudy so hard that it
raised a bruise on her cheek
before she ran away from
Jessie's cubicle. Jessie cackled

as Trudy screamed, "Crazy bitch!"

"Jessie Maracle, I'm giving you a spoken notice at this moment. You are being sent home without pay to reconsider your actions for 24 hours," Hank spoke from the speaker on her phone.

Jessie winced, such actions were the first step to a dismissal. It was policy to do it in private in the supervisor's office, not through the phone. She glanced around herself to see if anyone in the nearby cubicle noticed. She looked up to see that Ward the floor's security guard was at her door.

She picked up the phone and screamed into it, "You've called security! I can't believe you're such a pussy!"

The security guard took the receiver and put it back down for her. "I suggest you go home quietly, and call a mental health professional if you're having problems, Ms. Maracle. I'm not going to let you escalate your personal issues into workplace violence."

She snorted but got her things and left for the day. The guard escorted her to the parking lot.

She consoled herself by logging onto Rezgrrl when she got home. Only to see a debate was in progress over the transcript of her chat with Minnie Sparrow:

Minnie

Here is the free site evaluation you wanted.

I wish to congratulate you on entering the modern day and age and getting an addy and a website. You have taken a step into the brave new world outside of the Bush!

I see that most of the special events you are attending is pow-wows. You can use willow bark to cure the headaches that the steel drums gives the people in the grandstands...

And it got worse from there. Jessie wanted to crawl up into a hole to die. It was like she'd written the post when she was skunked! She glanced at the bottle of Liquid Courage on the shelf, and threw it into the garbage.

She didn't know where to begin to put things back together again, but her workplace had a 24/7 employee counseling support line. She looked up the number and started there. By the end of the week she was signed up to addiction services. She'd already stopped taking Liquid Courage, but they forced her to report to the detoxification clinic for regular check-ups.

She had to follow the rules the clinic gave her to keep her job. The fact that she was in an employee sponsored program meant she couldn't be fired even if her physical presence made the employees nervous.

She emailed Ashton that she was no longer working on Liquid Courage, and encouraged him to stop working on it too. All she got in return was a receipt that the email had been read.

She was no longer allowed to "self–medicate" with alcohol during her recovery. "Your glass or two wasn't so bad before Liquid Courage entered your life, but there's still the chance you'll have an adverse reaction with the residual amounts in your system if you imbibe now."

Two months later Hank forwarded Jessie and Ashton a

link to an online article about an incident of workplace violence at Liquid Courage's headquarters with the words, You are to cease all work on this account immediately!

All the employees for Liquid Courage were taking the pills, and it'd been hard to tell who was the shooter and the victim since they were equally belligerent to the SWAT team during the shooting. Liquid Courage was taken off the market, and the investigative reporter contended, Liquid Courage should have never been offered to the public. It's been credited with being a 'performance enhancer', but it generates the Dark Triad of psychopathic traits in its consumers. The formula was created in the 19th century and inspired the novel 'The Strange Case of Dr. Jekyll and Mr. Hyde'...

Jessie rebranded "Rezgrrl" as "Conscious Creation" now that she couldn't use alcohol for her brainstorming sessions. Her first project under the brand was to give Minnie Sparrow a free remake of her site, with better graphics, pages, and a blog that she could update on an as needed basis. Minnie had people ask her about the best medicines to use for alternative treatments in her comments section. It didn't always mean a direct sale, but it built her online reputation and credibility. She had more people seeking her out at the pow-wows she attended as a vendor. Minnie agreed that the new site was an improvement over the old one. She allowed Jessie to use screen captures of before and after pictures for Conscious Creation. Jessie made sure that her explanatory comments were more tactful when she explained her rationale about the necessary changes to the site.

Her coworkers didn't start to trust her until she turned in a series of compelling pitches for the Lucidity account. By the end of the year she was their "Miracle Worker" of ad campaigns again.

About Author

Cathy Smith is a Mohawk writer who lives on a Status Reservation on the Canadian Side of the Border.

You can follow her at:

Wordpress: bit.ly/2e41qWT

Facebook: bit.ly/2dP3rXd

Twitter: @khiatons

Instagram:@cathy2891

Tumblr: bit.ly/2G3dEjo

Pinterest: https://www.pinterest.com/Khiatons/

Tiktok: bit.ly/3KoGwBf

Sign up to the Cathy Smith-Khiatons-I Write Substack https://bit.ly/4qATMGH to receive news and excerpts of new publications and promotions.